D1243123

THE WUGGIE NORPLE STORY

by
DANIEL M. PINKWATER
PICTURES by
TOMIE dePAOLA

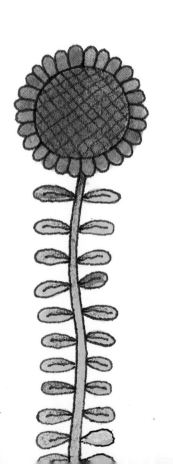

Library of Congress Cataloging in Publication Data

Pinkwater, Daniel Manus
  The Wuggie Norple story.

  *Summary: The family's new pet kitten grows at such a ridiculous
rate that the father must bring home animals to compare sizes each
day.*

  [1. Cats—Fiction.   2. Humorous stories]
I. De Paola, Thomas Anthony.   II. Title.
PZ7.P6335Wu   [E]   79-19014
                ISBN 0-590-07569-1

Published by Four Winds Press
A division of Scholastic Magazines, Inc., New York, N.Y.
Text copyright © 1980 by Daniel Pinkwater
Illustrations copyright © 1980 by Tomie de Paola

Printed in the United States of America
Library of Congress Catalog Card Number: 79-19014
   1 2 3 4 5 84 83 82 81 80

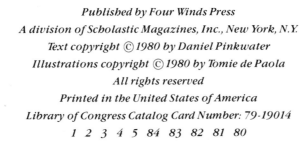

To Maestro Rohan E. Joseph

In a little house, in a little village, not far away from Thunderbolt City, lived a whistle fixer named Lunchbox Louie. He had a wife named Bigfoot the Chipmunk and a little son named King Waffle. Every day Lunchbox Louie would kiss Bigfoot the Chipmunk and King Waffle, and walk to his shop in Thunderbolt City.

Bigfoot the Chipmunk would wave good-bye to Lunchbox Louie until he was out of sight. Then she would sweep the floors, make the beds, and chop up onions for supper.

King Waffle would sit in the backyard hitting a big rock with a little hammer.

Some days King Waffle would walk with his mother, Bigfoot the Chipmunk, through the streets of the little village and out into the fields. Some days they would walk all the way to a little lake called Nosewort Pond. Bigfoot the Chipmunk would bring some food in a basket, and she and King Waffle would sit beside Nosewort Pond, eating a picnic lunch and playing with the wild caterpillars that lived there.

In the evening, Lunchbox Louie would come home from Thunderbolt City. Bigfoot the Chipmunk and King Waffle would be waiting in the doorway when he came up the road. Lunchbox Louie would always bring something from the city for Bigfoot the Chipmunk and King Waffle. Sometimes he would bring a coconut. Sometimes he would bring a pair of eyeglasses made out of candy. Once he brought a rubber turtle that danced on a string.

Bigfoot the Chipmunk would fry up the onions she had chopped that morning. After supper the family would sit outside the house and Lunchbox Louie would play tunes on a whistle he had made from a carrot.

One evening, when Lunchbox Louie came back from Thunderbolt City, he had a special present for King Waffle. It was a little orange kitten. King Waffle named the kitten Wuggie Norple.

When Lunchbox Louie came home that night he noticed something. He noticed that Wuggie Norple was a bigger kitten than she had been the day before. "She's as big as a bulldog," Lunchbox Louie said.

"She doesn't seem any bigger to me," Bigfoot the Chipmunk said. "Maybe you're still getting used to her."

The next morning, when Lunchbox Louie had left for his shop in Thunderbolt City, and Bigfoot the Chipmunk had waved good-bye until he was out of sight, after Bigfoot the Chipmunk had swept the floors and made the beds, and chopped up the onions for supper, King Waffle sat in the sun in the backyard, hitting the big rock with the little hammer, and Wuggie Norple pounced on his feet and played with his toes.

The next day, when Lunchbox Louie was about to leave to walk to his shop in Thunderbolt City, just before he kissed Bigfoot the Chipmunk and King Waffle good-bye, he looked at the cat, Wuggie Norple. He thought Wuggie Norple was a bigger cat than she had been the night before. "It seems to me that she is just a little bigger than a bulldog," Lunchbox Louie said.

"She seems the same size as before to me," Bigfoot the Chipmunk said. "Maybe you are not used to seeing her in the sunshine."

Lunchbox Louie walked away from the little house slowly. He walked away from the little village slowly. He walked toward Thunderbolt City slowly. He was thinking about Wuggie Norple, the orange cat, and how she seemed just a little bigger than a bulldog.

When Lunchbox Louie came home from Thunderbolt City that night he had something under his arm. Bigfoot the Chipmunk and King Waffle could see it a long way off. It was something big and white. When Lunchbox Louie got closer they could see that it was a bulldog. Lunchbox Louie put the bulldog down next to Wuggie Norple. "This is Freckleface Chilibean," Lunchbox Louie said. "As you can see, Freckleface Chilibean is a bulldog, and as you can see, Wuggie Norple is just a little bigger than he is. I hope you are satisfied."

"I think Freckleface Chilibean is a little bit bigger than Wuggie Norple," Bigfoot the Chipmunk said.

"They look about the same size to me," King Waffle said.

Wuggie Norple growled at Freckleface Chilibean,
and Freckleface Chilibean ran and hid under the sofa.

The next morning, when Lunchbox Louie was about to leave for his shop in Thunderbolt City, he said, "Wuggie Norple has grown during the night. Now anybody can see that she is bigger than Freckleface Chilibean. In fact she is almost as big as a six-year-old razorback hog."

"It does seem to me that Wuggie Norple is a tiny bit bigger than Freckleface Chilibean," Bigfoot the Chipmunk said.

"But she is nowhere near as big as a six-year-old razorback hog," King Waffle said.

Lunchbox Louie walked away from his little house slowly. He was thinking about Wuggie Norple, about how she was almost as big as a six-year-old razorback hog.

During the day Wuggie Norple made friends with Freckleface Chilibean, and they chased each other around the big rock while King Waffle sat hitting it with his little hammer.

That night, when Bigfoot the Chipmunk and King Waffle and Wuggie Norple and Freckleface Chilibean went to the door to wait for Lunchbox Louie to arrive home from Thunderbolt City, they could see that he was carrying something very heavy. He was walking slowly and stopping to rest every few steps. When he got closer they saw that he was carrying a big hog.

"This is Papercup Mixmaster," Lunchbox Louie said. "As you can see, Papercup Mixmaster is a six-year-old razorback hog, and as you can see, Wuggie Norple is almost as big as he is."

"Oh, Wuggie Norple isn't that big," Bigfoot the Chipmunk said.

"Wuggie Norple isn't even half as big," King Waffle said.

The next morning, Lunchbox Louie said, "Look! Wuggie Norple is bigger than Papercup Mixmaster!"

"Well, almost as big," Bigfoot the Chipmunk said.

"Maybe a tiny little bit bigger," King Waffle said.

"Bigger!" Lunchbox Louie shouted. "Bigger! Bigger! Bigger! She's as big as a young horse!"

Lunchbox Louie walked slowly away from the little house.

During the day King Waffle helped his mother Bigfoot the Chipmunk build a pen for Papercup Mixmaster.

That night, when Bigfoot the Chipmunk and King Waffle and Wuggie Norple and Freckleface Chilibean and Papercup Mixmaster went to the door to wait for Lunchbox Louie to come home from Thunderbolt City, they saw that he was carrying something very big and very heavy.

"This is Exploding Poptart," Lunchbox Louie said. "As you can see, Exploding Poptart is a young horse, and as you can see, Wuggie Norple is every bit as big as Exploding Poptart. I hope you are satisfied."

"Nonsense," said Bigfoot the Chipmunk. "A cat can't be as big as a young horse."

"Wuggie Norple isn't anywhere near as big as Exploding Poptart," King Waffle said.

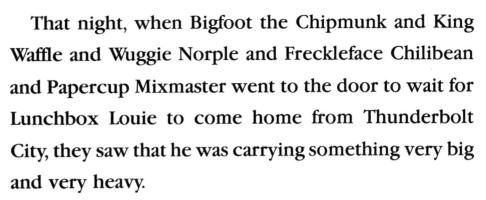

The next morning Lunchbox Louie said, "As I live and breathe, Wuggie Norple has gotten even bigger. She's even bigger than Exploding Poptart!"

"Not at all," said Bigfoot the Chipmunk.

"Not at all," said King Waffle.

"Not at all?" shouted Lunchbox Louie. "She's as big as an elephant. You'll see!"

During the day King Waffle rode Exploding Poptart around the backyard, Papercup Mixmaster snuffled and grunted in his pen, and Freckleface Chilibean and Wuggie Norple chased each other around the house.

In the evening, when Bigfoot the Chipmunk and King
Waffle and Wuggie Norple and Freckleface Chilibean
and Papercup Mixmaster and Exploding Poptart went
to the door to wait for Lunchbox Louie, they saw that
he was carrying something very very big, and gray.

"This is Laughing Gas Alligator," said Lunchbox Louie, who was all out of breath. "As you can see, Laughing Gas Alligator is an Indian Elephant, and as you can see, Wuggie Norple, the cat, is just exactly the same size as the elephant."

"You know, actually, they do seem to be about the same size," said Bigfoot the Chipmunk.

"They are exactly the same size," said King Waffle.

"Well, finally!" said Lunchbox Louie.

The next day was Saturday, and Lunchbox Louie didn't have to go to work, so he took Bigfoot the Chipmunk, and King Waffle, and Wuggie Norple, and Freckleface Chilibean, and Papercup Mixmaster, and Exploding Poptart, and Laughing Gas Alligator, and a big basket of lunch, and they all went to Nosewort Pond for a picnic.